Edgar, Allan, and Poe
and the
Tell-Tale Beets

written by
natalie rompella

illustrated by
françois ruyer

Lobster Press™

Edgar, Allan, and Poe, and the Tell-Tale Beets
Text © 2009 Natalie Rompella
Illustrations © 2009 François Ruyer

Published by Lobster Press™
1620 Sherbrooke Street West, Suites C & D
Montréal, Québec   H3H 1C9
Tel. (514) 904-1100 • Fax (514) 904-1101
www.lobsterpress.com

Publisher: Alison Fripp
Editor: Meghan Nolan
Graphic Design & Production: Tammy Desnoyers
Production Assistant: Leslie Mechanic

Library and Archives Canada Cataloguing in Publication

Rompella, Natalie, 1974-
    Edgar, Allan, and Poe, and the tell-tale beets / Natalie Rompella ; François Ruyer, illustrator.

ISBN 978-1-897550-17-5 (bound). ISBN 978-1-897550-28-1 (pbk.)

    I. Ruyer, François II. Title.

PS3618.0656E34 2009   jC813'.6   C2009-900098-9

Printed and bound in China.

To Bun,
May you never try to hide your food – I know all the tricks!

– Natalie Rompella

It all began with the beets.
The revoltingly red beets that drove Edgar, Allan,
and Poe to do the horrible thing they did.

And so begins the tale ... the tale of the beating beets ...

The three boys lived in a rickety old house.
It often reeked from the odd meals their mother served.

"You can have dessert only if you finish your dinner,"
their mother said. Oh, the moans, the groans,
that came from Edgar, Allan, and Poe.

Edgar did not like the squishy squash their mother served. Allan despised the liquidy liver that still looked alive. Bouncy balls of brussels sprouts made Poe want to barf.

But they especially hated beets. Beets were so red, so slimy, and so hard to hide. Edgar, Allan, and Poe often got no dessert.

Until ... the three boys discovered a loose floorboard underneath Poe's chair.

Wednesday night at dinner, the family sat down
for meatloaf and a big helping of beets.

"I have a plan," Edgar whispered to his brothers.
"I will get Mother and Father's attention. Allan, you will
grab our disgusting dinner, and Poe, you will put it under
the floorboard." The two other boys nodded.

"Oh my goodness," began Edgar, "what do I see at the window but a giant wearing an Elvis wig!"

Allan stabbed all three helpings of beets onto his fork.

Poe lifted the loose floorboard. The beets slipped into the hole with a splosh. Poe quietly replaced the floorboard.

"What great appetites you have!" exclaimed their mother. "As a reward for finishing your meals, you each get a big bowl of banana pudding!"

Thursday night, liver and brussels sprouts were served. Allan shivered in disgust.

"Oh, me, oh, my! What is that I see on the lawn?" questioned Edgar. "Could it possibly be an alien in a clown suit?"

The liver languished and the brussels sprouts bounced as Allan dropped them into the hole under Poe's chair.

"My boys! You ate it all! You each get a thick slab of chocolate cake!" their mother said, clapping her hands together in delight.

Friday night, their father ladled cold cucumber soup and squash into each of their bowls. "By golly! A dragon is eating your prize-winning rosebush, Father!" Edgar said as he pointed at the window.

The soup spattered and the squash squished into the hole.
Allan had to use his toes to hide all the strings the squash
left around the edge of the floorboard.

"You boys never cease to amaze me!" their mother laughed. "Oatmeal-raisin cookies for each of you!"

Saturday morning, as the boys ate their pancakes (which they actually liked), Poe began to notice a funny smell. "Something stinks," he said. His parents couldn't smell a thing.

"Why, that's probably from the giant removing his shoes," Edgar began. "Giants have big stinky feet." He kicked Allan and Poe under the table. They nodded.

As the boys finished their breakfast,
they faintly heard a *Beet, Beet. Beet, Beet.*

By lunch, the smell was overwhelming.
"Peeuuuw!" exclaimed Allan.

Their mother raised her nose in the air. "I don't smell anything."

"The alien is probably living in the house," started Edgar as
he gave Allan the evil eye. "Aliens don't own toothbrushes."

The boys thought they heard a quiet *Beet, Beet. Liver, Liver,* but they weren't sure.

At dinner, the three boys had to wear clothespins on their noses to keep from smelling the awful stench. "What ever are you three doing?" their mother asked.

"Covering our noses from
the awful smell!" cried Poe
as he ran out of the room for fresh air.
Their mother looked at their father, confused.

"The dragon is probably burping up
stinky roses," explained Edgar.

None of the boys even finished their pizza, which was their favorite. As they left the table, they softly heard, *Beet, Beet. Liver, Liver. Brussels, Brussels,* but they ignored it.

Sunday morning, the family sat down for breakfast, the boys' faces green from the smell. The boys' mother slopped oatmeal into their bowls. They hated oatmeal. Edgar looked at Allan; Allan looked at Poe; Poe looked at Edgar.

Edgar poked Allan to remove the floorboard ...

"Stop! I can't take it anymore!"
shouted Poe. "The beating! The beating of the beets!
We've buried them under the floorboard with all
the other awful dishes we've been served!"

Poe bent down to show their parents what he was
talking about and ...
Beet, Beet. Liver, Liver. Brussels, Brussels.
Soup, Soup. Squash, Squash.

Suddenly, wood splintered as the mixture spewed out like
a geyser. No longer were there beets, cucumber soup,
and liver – now there was a large blob that smelled like a
moose with brussels sprout breath. It spun through the air.

The whole family watched until down it came, landing splat on Edgar, who, just before it hit, opened his mouth to shriek.

The mixture covered his hair in a stringy, chunky, drippy
mess that jiggled when he shook his head. A large bubbly
blob clung to his right earlobe like an enormous earring.
Edgar spit out what had landed in his mouth,
let out a cheese-curdling scream,
and ran to his room.

At dinner that night, the boys ate every awful scrap on their plates, including the yucky yams with a parsley garnish. Needless to say, they did not get dessert for quite some time.

Edgar, Allan, and Poe's father fixed the loose floorboard under Poe's chair and under every other chair in the house.

Except, however, one floorboard.
A floorboard *someone's* peas
were hidden under.